I CAN READ ABOUT

PAUL BUNYAN

Written by J.I. Anderson
Illustrated by Joel Snyder

Troll Associates

The Great Lakes are *great!* The Mississippi River is *long!* The Grand Canyon is *huge*, and the Rocky Mountains are *big!*

Some storytellers say that they were the work of one man . . . a very *big* man named Paul Bunyan.

Paul Bunyan was the biggest
and the best lumberjack in America—
the best there ever was.

S-W-O-O-S-H!

He was so strong that he could chop
down an entire forest with one
swing of his mighty axe.

Paul was born big. Some people say he was the biggest baby
ever born in the state of Maine.

He caused lots of problems!

Sometimes, when he sneezed, he blew
people clear out of the state.

"When I grow up, I'm going to be a lumberjack,"
he said.
In those days, the forests were thick with
trees.
"T-I-M-B-E-R!" he called
as he chopped down trees.
"T-I-M-B-E-R!"

And sure enough, when he did grow up, he set out
to be a lumberjack. By this time, he was
awfully big. So big, in fact, that
he decided to go to Michigan
and open his own logging
camp.

What a group he hired!
He got the very best crew he could find . . . over two thousand
people. There were all sorts of folks in his camp!
Johnny Inkslinger was the bookkeeper.
Sourdough Sam was the cook.
And Hals Halvorsen was
the foreman.

There was work to be done.
Paul did things in a big way.

His camp was the biggest
and best in the country. It
was so big that Paul had to dig the
Great Lakes—just to have water
for the crew.

Paul invented modern tools to help the men with their work—
tools like the two-man saw, and the grindstone for
sharpening axes. He also invented special sleds
for carrying logs from the forest to the camp.

By golly, what a place!

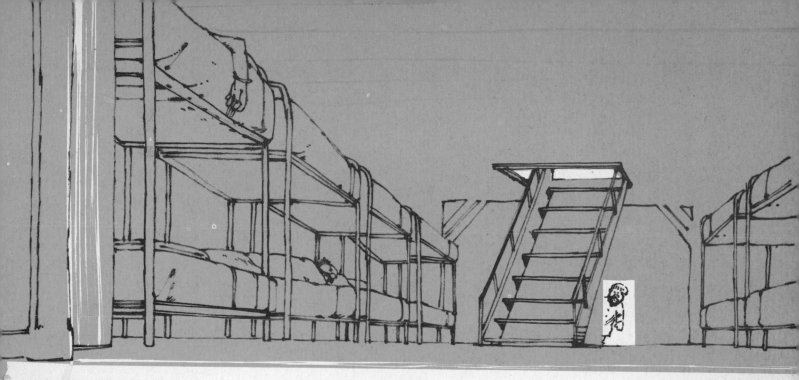

The bunkhouse in Paul's camp was so big
that the men needed maps to find their beds at night.

And talk about *big* eaters . . .
Every morning Sourdough Sam had a *big* job to do. He had to cook enough pancakes for all the men. He cooked and cooked and cooked . . . thousands and thousands of pancakes.

The camp hummed with the sounds of work.
People came and went. There was a lot to do.
But sometimes Paul was lonely. Sometimes he wished that
he had a friend his size to help him.

Then, one winter day—during the winter of the blue snow—
Paul found just the friend he was looking for.

Something was buried in the snow.
"Who's there?" Paul asked.
"MOOOOOO . . . . ," came the reply.

It was a baby, blue ox!

Paul picked up the ox and carried it back to camp. He nursed the ox until it was strong and healthy.
Paul decided to name the ox Babe.

Babe grew quickly, and before long he was almost as big
as Paul . . . which caused problems.

One day, Babe knocked over a tank of water. The entire camp might have drowned, but Paul acted quickly. As fast as he could, he dug a ditch to let the water drain away.

Today, that "ditch" is called
the Mississippi River.

Even if he *did* knock over things, Babe was a great help
to Paul. Working together, the two of them were able
to do more work in a single day than all the others
could do in a year. In fact, they worked so hard,
there was no more work to be done.
Paul had to close the camp.

"Let's go see the country, Babe," said Paul. "I want to see the trees called redwoods—the trees that grow taller than the sky." On the way west, Paul and Babe stopped in logging camps and helped the men with their work.

In Wisconsin, they saw a group of men trying to pull logs up a twisted, crooked road.

"Let's help," said Paul.

"Let's straighten out that road."
Then Paul hitched Babe to one end of the road.
Babe snorted, and puffed, and pulled. Suddenly, there was a loud
CRACK and a loud SNAP! One by one, the curves snapped straight
until the road was perfect.
"Hooray," shouted the loggers.
"Three cheers for Paul and Babe."

Paul and Babe explored America. Everywhere they went, people were happy to see them. They helped the settlers in North Dakota clear the land for their farms.

In Montana, they dug lakes and streams so the people would have fresh water.

And in Iowa they helped the farmers plant corn.

In Arizona, Paul accidentally dragged his pick on the ground. The place where his pick cut into the ground is still there today. It's called the Grand Canyon.

In Washington, Babe stepped on some hills
and made the Cascade Mountains.
And when Paul spilled a glass of water,
he made the Puget Sound.

Once when Paul burned some hot biscuits, he
tossed them away.
They were too hard to eat. But where they landed are
the Rocky Mountains today.

Paul and Babe roamed all over America.

Some people say they saw Paul and Babe
heading for Alaska. And still others say
that Paul and Babe became cowboys in Texas.

But wherever they are,
some day soon . . .
it's just possible . . .
that you might see . . .

. . . Paul Bunyan and his great blue ox.